Put Beginning Readers on the Right 1
ALL ABOARD READING™

The All Aboard Reading series is especially designed for beginning readers. Written by noted authors and illustrated in full color, these are books that children really want to read—books to excite their imagination, expand their interests, make them laugh, and support their feelings. With fiction and nonfiction stories that are high interest and curriculum-related, All Aboard Reading books offer something for every young reader. And with four different reading levels, the All Aboard Reading series lets you choose which books are most appropriate for your children and their growing abilities.

Picture Readers
Picture Readers have super-simple texts, with many nouns appearing as rebus pictures. At the end of each book are 24 flash cards—on one side is a rebus picture; on the other side is the written-out word.

Station Stop 1
Station Stop 1 books are best for children who have just begun to read. Simple words and big type make these early reading experiences more comfortable. Picture clues help children to figure out the words on the page. Lots of repetition throughout the text helps children to predict the next word or phrase—an essential step in developing word recognition.

Station Stop 2
Station Stop 2 books are written specifically for children who are reading with help. Short sentences make it easier for early readers to understand what they are reading. Simple plots and simple dialogue help children with reading comprehension.

Station Stop 3
Station Stop 3 books are perfect for children who are reading alone. With longer text and harder words, these books appeal to children who have mastered basic reading skills. More complex stories captivate children who are ready for more challenging books.

In addition to All Aboard Reading books, look for All Aboard Math Readers™ (fiction stories that teach math concepts children are learning in school); All Aboard Science Readers™ (nonfiction books that explore the most fascinating science topics in age-appropriate language); All Aboard Poetry Readers™ (funny, rhyming poems for readers of all levels); and All Aboard Mystery Readers™ (puzzling tales where children piece together evidence with the characters).

All Aboard for happy reading!

GROSSET & DUNLAP
Published by the Penguin Group
Penguin Group (USA) Inc., 375 Hudson Street, New York, New York 10014, U.S.A.
Penguin Group (Canada), 90 Eglinton Avenue East, Suite 700, Toronto, Ontario,
Canada M4P 2Y3 (a division of Pearson Penguin Canada Inc.)
Penguin Books Ltd, 80 Strand, London WC2R 0RL, England
Penguin Ireland, 25 St Stephen's Green, Dublin 2, Ireland
(a division of Penguin Books Ltd)
Penguin Group (Australia), 250 Camberwell Road, Camberwell, Victoria 3124, Australia
(a division of Pearson Australia Group Pty Ltd)
Penguin Books India Pvt Ltd, 11 Community Centre, Panchsheel Park, New Delhi - 110 017, India
Penguin Group (NZ), 67 Apollo Drive, Mairangi Bay, Auckland 1311, New Zealand
(a division of Pearson New Zealand Ltd)
Penguin Books (South Africa) (Pty) Ltd, 24 Sturdee Avenue, Rosebank,
Johannesburg 2196, South Africa

Penguin Books Ltd, Registered Offices:
80 Strand, London WC2R 0RL, England

Angelina Ballerina © 2007 Helen Craig Ltd. (illustrations) and Katharine Holabird (text).
The Angelina Ballerina name and character and the dancing Angelina logo are trademarks
of HIT Entertainment Limited, Katharine Holabird and Helen Craig Ltd., Reg. U.S. Pat. & Tm.
Off. All rights reserved. Published by Grosset & Dunlap, a division of Penguin Young Readers
Group, 345 Hudson Street, New York, New York 10014. ALL ABOARD READING and GROSSET
& DUNLAP are trademarks of Penguin Group (USA) Inc. Printed in the U.S.A.

Library of Congress Cataloging-in-Publication Data

Holabird, Katharine.
Angelina's silly little sister / by Katharine Holabird ; based on the illustrations by Helen Craig.
p. cm. — (All aboard reading. Station stop 1) (Angelina Ballerina)
Summary: Polly always seems to get in the way when Angelina and Alice want to play
alone, and so they agree to play hide-and-seek with her but then leave her in her hiding
place while they play inside.
ISBN 978-0-448-44468-0 (pbk.)
[1. Sisters—Fiction. 2. Hide-and-seek—Fiction. 3. Mice—Fiction.] I. Craig, Helen, ill. II. Title.
PZ7.H689Aq 2007
[E]—dc22
2006024790

10 9 8 7 6 5 4 3

Angelina's Silly Little Sister

By Katharine Holabird
Based on the illustrations by Helen Craig

Grosset & Dunlap

This is Angelina's little sister.
Her name is Polly.

Polly follows Angelina
everywhere.

This is Angelina's best friend.

Her name is Alice.

Every day they play together

after school.

Angelina and Alice like to dance.

Polly wants to dance, too.

But she can't remember the steps!

Angelina and Alice
do cartwheels.

Polly tries to do the same thing.

But she wobbles and falls over!

Today the two mouselings

have a pink tea party.

Polly wants to join.

"Please, I won't spill.

I promise," says Polly.

Ooops! Polly spills the tea

and makes a horrible mess!

Angelina and Alice go inside.

Angelina tells Polly,

"Alice and I want to
play alone now."

"WAAAA!" screams Polly.

Mrs. Mouseling hears Polly.

She gives Polly a hug.

She says to Angelina,

"Please play with Polly
a little longer.

I am making a cheesecake."

Angelina stomps

into the garden with Alice.

Polly skips after them.

"I want to play hide-and-seek,"
Polly tells them.

All at once,

Angelina has an idea.

She whispers in Alice's ear.

"Okay. I'll be it,"
Angelina tells Polly.
"Yippee yay!" shouts Polly.

Angelina counts to ten:
"One . . . two . . . three . . .
four . . . five . . . six . . .
seven . . . eight . . . nine . . .
TEN!
Ready or not,
here I come!"
Angelina shouts.

Alice is only pretending to hide.
She is behind the garden shed.
"I found you!" Angelina shouts
so Polly can hear.

Angelina points to the apple tree.

"Polly always hides there,"

she whispers.

"Now we can play by ourselves."

Angelina and Alice run
into the house.
They dress up like ballerinas
and dance around the bedroom.
They forget all about Polly.

After a while,

they begin to get hungry.

They smell the cheesecake.

"Let's have our pink tea party

now," suggests Alice.

"First we have to get my sister,"

says Angelina.

Angelina and Alice look
behind the apple tree.
Polly's not there!
"Oh, no!" cries Angelina.
"Where has Polly gone?"

Angelina and Alice
search everywhere,
even under the wheelbarrow

and behind the bushes.
Still no Polly!

Angelina is very upset
and runs into the kitchen.
"I lost Polly!" Angelina cries.
"I was not a good big sister.
I didn't want her playing with us."

Mrs. Mouseling gives
Angelina a hug.
"Don't worry," she says kindly.
"Polly fell asleep
under the apple tree.
So I put her to bed."

Angelina races upstairs.

She is so glad to see

her little sister!

"Are you ready for cake?" she asks.

"Yum!" says Polly.

Mrs. Mouseling's
cheesecake is yummy.
Everyone has a lovely time
at the pink tea party.
Especially Polly.

"I will help you pour the tea,"
Angelina says.

"You are a good big sister,"
says Polly.
And this time she spills only
a little bit.